YOU RUIN IT WHEN YOU TALK

A novelette

SARAH MANVEL

●PEN PEN

First Published in 2020
by Open Pen, 25 Crescent Road, London, E13 0LU

openpen.co.uk

9781916413689

OPNOV008

OPEN PEN NOVELETTES #7
"You Ruin It When You Talk"
First Edition
© Sarah Manvel, 2020

He bumped into me to interrupt the guy I was talking to and asked for his rolling papers. The guy handed them over and I ended up holding his pint while he made the cigarette. Somehow we got on to movies. When I said I was over superhero stuff, he scoffed and asked who my five favourite directors are.

This was disappointing, but you're supposed to give people a chance. Besides, the first two were easy: Jane Campion and Andrea Arnold. I don't think he'd heard of them because he didn't ask any questions. I thought out loud a little, then said Peter Weir, who at least he'd heard of, but clearly had never seen any of his films. He kept sneering, and I kept pretending he was engaging in good faith. For my fourth I said Jean-Pierre Jeunet, even though *Amélie* is so problematic it's tough to love, but then I corrected my choice to Doug Liman, who changed action movies completely but weirdly doesn't get the credit.

He wanted to debate me on that, but didn't know enough about the difference between Liman's Bourne and the Greengrass Bournes, and he hadn't even heard of *Go*. And then I realised that was my main criterion for a favourite director: someone who can change a genre completely. That meant my fifth choice was obviously Catherine Hardwicke, who gave Oscar Isaac his first leading role, and who trailblazed young-adult cinema

1

with *Twilight*, which is an objectively fantastic film.

But before I could say why, he laughed at me. He said it was a terrible film full of terrible actors. I said he was wrong. When he realised I was completely sincere he said, "You should go back to him. You know, your husband?"

"What? What husband?"

"The guy who gave me the rollies."

"I just met him there now. Right before you."

He said, "You two suit each other," and turned away.

o

We were in Farringdon going through the second-date motions, asking about siblings and jobs and when we moved to London.

"I moved down from Scotland for a girl," he said. "We lived together for six years till we broke up."

"That's a long time to live with someone."

"Mm. Well, there were problems from the start. In the six years we lived together we never had sex."

I set down my cheesy chip. "What?"

"Oh yeah, it was horrible. And after a few years it really started to bother me."

o

We'd messaged a bit through the dating app before

he asked for my number. When I said my only rule on getting back out there was not giving anyone my number until we'd met in person, he invited me on a date in a bar in Leicester Square. When I arrived he was already seated in the outdoor area with a cocktail.

When I said I would go get my drink he insisted I sit down and he would pay for it. While he failed to attract the attention of a waiter, I decided to lighten the mood by asking why he'd picked the place.

"For starters, it has excellent CCTV."

o

I was in a ghastly club with some colleagues. A swiftie had turned into a session and the brick shithouse from my team had paid everybody's entrance fee, so we'd carried on. It was fun, dancing, but then I accidentally made eye contact with this dude. He leaped over and swept me around the dance floor with his hands on my arse while bombarding me with questions: what was my name, where did I live, what was a pretty woman like me doing in a place like this. I was taken aback but you're supposed to give people a chance.

"Oh," he said then. "I love your tongue."

o

The date in the Southbank Centre was fine, nothing spectacular. I checked my messages in the app when I got home and was surprised to see something from him already.

He said he'd had a lovely time and couldn't wait to see me again, and he would be in touch once he'd organised the delivery of his new refrigerator.

o

It was late and I had my earbuds in at the bus stop. Next to me a pair of teenagers were alternately snogging and giggling. They were impossibly charming. They were so taken with each other, so clearly deeply in love, that the entire waiting area was smiling indulgently at them.

Her bus pulled up and they made an emotional farewell. As she was going upstairs, the boy knocked on the bus's windscreen until he got the driver's attention.

"Busman? You take care of her, yeah? You get her home safe. She's precious cargo."

o

I finished taking off my clothes and turned to him with a smile.

"Oh my God," the Scot said. "You have the most fantastic eyebrows."

I sucked in my breath as he continued, "No, I am serious, woman. Look at those. Do you go to a salon?"

"No," I said. "I grew them myself."

o

In the two hours we spent together he did not ask me one single question. I had bought the first round of drinks, and by the time I was halfway through my pint I was fizzy with anticipating how he'd manage buying his.

When the time came, he stood up. "I suppose I should buy you a drink," he said, then looked at the glass in my hand.

He looked at that glass until I gave up. "Same again."

o

He thought telling me about the time he punched a woman in the face outside a club was a funny story.

o

The date in Camden was going well until I asked where he lived.

He stammered, then proceeded to tell me how he had interviewed to live on a houseboat as the

5

fifth roommate to four abstemious incestuous vegan lesbians. Incestuous only in that during the interview they had made it clear who was exes with who, and then he told me all about who he thought was sleeping with each other anyway. Them being teetotal was not a problem, and he had guessed he could live with the lesbian drama, but he hadn't been prepared to tolerate the veganism.

This was all extremely interesting, but hadn't answered my question.

He made a face. Well, as it happened, when he last came back from Burning Man, he had been shocked to realise how much of his lovely money he was expected to spend on rent. He simply couldn't justify it. So he had a van parked in a mate's driveway in Tottenham, and the mate let him use the bogs if necessary (although one of the benefits of being a man, he said, is you can just piss anywhere) and he showered at the gym.

I tried very hard not to make a face myself but he said, "See, this is why I didn't want to tell you. It looks like you're judging me."

"Oh, I'm not judging you," I said. "I'm just thinking about my shower."

o

She showed up wearing a fleece.

o

The date in Borough Market was going well until he mentioned he'd recently decided to be exclusive with his girlfriend.

I covered my mouth, then uncovered it. "So what are you doing out with me?"

He waved his hands around. "We're having a nice time, aren't we?"

I got my jacket. "Are you gonna choose me over her?"

He stuttered, but I cut him off and said, "Then not enough."

o

It was my birthday and the work fancy surprised me in the kitchen. "Happy birthday!" he said and put his hands on my shoulders. "I hope this isn't inappropriate," he added, pulled me to him, and kissed me.

I went bright red, and he laughed and released me.

"You know," I managed, "if you really cared, you'd buy me an island."

o

We went to her choice of restaurant in Crystal Palace,

where she spent a long time explaining her food sensitivities to me and then the waiter. She then began explaining how she was trying to get her flat adapted, which was obviously very difficult and involved a lot of stress and trouble, but the works were necessary so that she could apply to be a foster mother in order to supplement her income.

You're supposed to give people a chance, so I asked why her income needed supplementing.

It turned out she was the bookkeeper for a chain of shops, a good job except her wages were awful since the owner was a terrible miser who never paid any of his bills properly. But she knew how to handle him. "Whenever he kicks off, I just tell him not to be so Jewish."

o

I met a friend for a drink in the ICA. When it was my turn to go to the bar I stood up. He said, "Oh my God. You're wearing a skirt."

"I am!" I said. "Don't I look good?"

"Don't ask me about women's fashion," he said. "I only care if it's easy to push up or pull down."

o

We met at Covent Garden station, but once the greetings were over he couldn't think of anywhere to go. I suggested one of the Masonic pubs since they are always quiet and certain to give him, if not me, decent service. So we walked up Long Acre and on arrival he bought me a pint and an orange juice for himself. As he finished paying, I took a huge swig and said, "I'm really sorry, but I needed that, it's been a rotten day at work," and he said, "Oh, I completely understand. I've also had a terrible time at work lately. For example, I was recently accused of being a paedophile."

o

He asked to meet at the doughnut truck in a street food market which, based on his name and this choice, made me think he was probably Muslim. As soon as we'd sat down with our coffees he merrily confirmed this, then added it was important he mention that up front because his mother had decided it was time for him to settle down with a nice Muslim girl. But we were having a fine time, chatting away, and it turned out he had once worked in a part of London where I used to live, so we swapped neighbourhood gossip until he brought the conversation back to how important his faith was to him.

I excused myself to the loo, mostly to wonder how I

was going to let him down.

When I came back, he was putting down his phone. "What a shame, you just missed my mum," he said. "She just called to see how this was going. You could have said hello to her. Would you like another coffee?"

o

I walked into the Christmas party and the Romanian girl from marketing said, "Oh wow. This is the first time I've seen you look pretty."

o

We were hanging out in the Scot's flat, nothing special except it was my first time there. We'd had enough wine that he decided to get some of his whisky down. He'd put up special shelves near the ceiling to display his collection. The bottles were arranged alphabetically, and a card covered with tasting notes was tied to each neck with string. I was willing to learn, but it soon turned into a lecture about how feminine palates couldn't properly appreciate the nuances of the flavours.

Then he changed the topic to one of his very best friends, a wee daftie. He, the daftie, had recently left a rambling drunken voicemail with a lot of singing in it, which the Scot played for me in full. Once he stopped laughing, which he did so much he didn't notice that I hadn't, he told me about the chat they'd had the week before. The wee daftie had had a date with a wee lassie, who was actually a much older woman, but hadn't mentioned it since. To be a good friend, the Scot had asked about it. But the wee daftie said it wasn't great.

"And when a man says that about sex, you know it's absolutely shocking. 'That bad?'

'Like a cheese toastie.'"

o

I agreed to go back to his mostly because I was curious to see his place. He'd spent the night telling me how he had given up his job to focus on his DJing career, a remarkable choice for someone in their mid-30s. I was hoping the clues to his family money would be lying around like pirate treasure but alas. I tried to make the most of it until he sat up and looked deeply into my eyes.

"You know what I would like?" he said. "If you paid attention to Mr Wiggly."

o

He began a litany against his ex-wife, which I interrupted

because you're supposed to give people a chance.

He smiled in a way that made it obvious the whole speech was rehearsed. "Well, it would never have worked out, you know, getting married was a terrible mistake. We were far too young."

"Really?" I sipped my drink. "I was twenty-three when I got married and I don't regret it at all. How old were you?"

He looked at his shoes. "Thirty-four."

o

I met her through friends, who had hinted she might have a problem with social cues. So when I decided to ask her out, I knew I had to be extra clear. I looked up the schedule for the upcoming gay film festival and found the showing of a movie about a young woman's struggle to accept her sexual identity. I sent her the link, she accepted, I bought the tickets, we saw it, it was good, and I was so confident things were going well I practically sprinted to the bar afterwards.

When I brought our drinks outside, she looked up at me. "You know, I was really surprised someone like you would take me to see this. What makes you interested in a movie about lesbians?"

It took me a moment to understand what was

happening. But the last thing I wanted to do was embarrass her, so I necked down a third of my pint and pulled back my chair. "I'm just really into film."

o

He suggested we meet in an artisanal cocktail bar in Dalston, which I had some trouble finding. We discussed the artisanal cocktail menu in detail before the waitress came over. I chose an artisanal cocktail she recommended and he chose sparkling water. That was a surprise after all this trouble and fuss and he said, "Oh, I don't drink. But I picked this place because your profile said you do. I wanted you to be comfortable."

o

At the interval, while my friend went to join the queue for the ladies, I checked my phone. There was a barrage of texts from a number I didn't recognise. Who had gotten around my only rule? The messages were detailed, and imaginative. And there were photos. The signal was bad so I had to wait for them to download. Once they did, I dropped my phone. I recognised the sender. Well, his face, anyway. It was the teenage son of another friend. I deleted the pics as fast as I could but I saw so much. Too much. This was a nightmare. What was I going to do?

Then I thought back to my last conversation with his mother. She'd mentioned he'd started seeing a girl in his sixth form. He was quite taken with her. His first proper girlfriend. An absolute sweetheart – oh my God – with the same name as me.

I laughed so hard other people in the gods turned to stare. I laughed so long that when my friend came back with our ice cream, she said she could hear me in the stairwell.

o

He insisted on walking me to the station. There it transpired we were traveling in the same direction, so he insisted on accompanying me onto the platform. Once there he swung me into a kiss I was unprepared for, and when he stuck his tongue into my mouth, I pushed him away.

"Dude. What are you doing?"

He stopped. "I don't know."

"Well until you do know, you shouldn't kiss me."

He started to splutter, then set his mouth in a way I didn't like. A train – not the right one – was pulling in. I got on it.

o

I was buying some veg at the Saturday market. The trader was making my change when an arm holding a giant courgette appeared from under the stall.

"Could you use a courgette, Nan?" the young owner of the arm said as she stood up.

The trader handed me my shrapnel and turned to her. "I'm sure I could, love, but things aren't as bad as all that."

The granddaughter laughed and waggled the courgette. "Oh, but it's a big 'un, Nan, you could have a fine old night with that."

The trader reached for the customer behind me. "I'm sure I could. I'd dice it and fry it in garlic butter."

o

The chat wasn't going well so I asked for his thoughts on enthusiastic consent.

He said he hoped he'd never need it himself but of course it should be available as a last resort.

It took me ages to work out that he thought I'd asked about euthanasia.

o

My landlady arranged to come over. I had lived there peacefully for a few years, so I thought we got on all right.

She spent an hour pointing out all the things I

had 'damaged' – all of which were, even if I do say so, reasonable wear and tear. She said that, due to all this 'damage', she would have to have the flat redecorated. I wouldn't have to move out while the works were going on although obviously I would have to live with the inconvenience. And since I had caused the 'damage', obviously I had to pay for it. Put all this in writing, I said. No problem, she said. Of course you agree, she said, once it's all done I'll obviously have to put the rent up.

She left and I lay on the floor a while. The Scot texted to see if I was free that night and when I was over at his I explained how I needed to get out, and fast.

"You could always move in here," he said.

o

I told the story of the dude who loved my tongue to someone I thought was a friend. She couldn't understand what my tongue had been doing.

"It was minding its business in my mouth."

"Well it had to be doing something. People don't normally act like this."

"They do to me," I said.

And she said, "Well, they would."

o

I met him in a bar in Bayswater. There'd been a few important meetings that day so I was dressed up and wearing my favourite necklace. We got our drinks and found a table. After a little chitchat, he said he liked my necklace.

"Thank you," I said.

"And I'm really glad you wore it," he said, "otherwise I'd have had nothing to compliment."

o

Sitting opposite each other on the DLR were a dishevelled older man and a younger man openly drinking a beer. The dishevelled man leaned across the aisle and asked the time. The drinker looked at his phone and said, "It is four minutes past two."

The dishevelled man said, "Already?"

o

The brick shithouse offered me the share of his taxi after a night out. I thought nothing of saying yes, seeing as we were mates, he knew I knew he was married and neither of us was particularly drunk.

I have rarely experienced such enthusiasm. It was like sharing a bathtub with an octopus made of puppies.

o

He said, "I think men should be like loo roll, strong and thoroughly absorbing."

I said, "Mmm yeah, but mostly not completely full of shit."

o

The crisis that day was such that I had to bring some work home with me. The Scot moped around. I guess he was annoyed I couldn't entertain him but didn't want to say so. After a while he asked if there was anything he could do. I said yes, make supper.

To my surprise, he agreed, and popped out to the shop. He came back and made a huge racket in the kitchen. Of course he used every single one of the pans. But I didn't find that out until later. Eventually, he called me over and I saved my work and came into the sitting room. Two plates were on the coffee table; each had a pork chop, baked beans and potatoes. My chop was a little burned, the potatoes were underdone and there was no butter or seasoning, but I didn't have time to care, I just wolfed it down. I stood up and thanked him, and he said, "That'll be £1.87."

"Excuse me?"

"Don't worry, I didn't charge you for the vegetables."

"I've cooked you dinner more than once."

And he said, "Well that was your own look-out."

o

The chat had gone well enough that I was pleased when he asked me out. We'd agreed on the details when he asked if I was planning to wear heels.

You're supposed to give people a chance, so I asked what that was about.

He texted back that he'd done the maths and, based on the height mentioned in my profile, if I wore heels on the date then I'd be taller than him. "And I know how that makes some women uncomfortable."

I texted back, "What makes this woman uncomfortable is a man she's never met telling her what to wear."

"I'm just trying to help," was the reply, so I blocked him.

o

We'd been mutuals online a while before arranging to meet up in person. I'd thought it wasn't a date, but I was wrong. He spent the first pint telling me how hard it was adjusting to life in London, but at least it was better for dating. The best thing about the dating scene in London, he said, was that people didn't overshare.

They didn't see dating as just a chance to complain. It was about connecting with people. In London everyone has their own personality, and everyone else respects that. And then he asked if I wanted a second pint.

"Sure," I said.

When he came back, he asked if I was divorced. "Yes," I said.

"Me too," he said.

I took a sip.

"It was because of our fertility problems," he said. "My ex has a hostile uterus."

o

I was invited to meet up in Soho with some film people I knew. When I arrived and saw I was the only woman, my heart sank. But even that would have been fine if the men hadn't decided to test my bona fides. But you're supposed to give people a chance, so I held my own even as the entire group started insulting me for refusing to agree that the Marvel Cinematic Universe is the greatest thing ever. I pretended they were engaging in good faith until one said that females couldn't appreciate the comic book formula. When I retorted, "I'm not a baby, I don't need formula," they angled their chairs away.

Except for one. He took it upon himself to explain

the metaphor of the superhero. And I let him, because otherwise I would have had to tell him his flies were down.

O

A friend from work brought me with her to a party in Hackney. He joined us as she was telling a funny story about relieving a schoolmate of his virginity. He was a redhead – as with Charlie Brown, redheads are my weakness – and sweet, or so it seemed as we got drunk together. As the night continued and my friend disappeared, I asked if he wanted to take me home.

With pleasure, he said, only he lived with his mother.

Fine, I said, we could go back to mine. Did he want to order an Uber?

No, he said, he didn't have the money for a taxi.

Whatever, I said. We'll get a night bus.

Once we were seated, he said, "I should probably warn you. It's been a while, so it's going to be bad."

It took me a moment. "Wait. Wait a minute. Why should I sleep with you if it's going to be bad?"

We proceeded to have an unseemly row on this night bus. I thought he might talk about how intimidatingly beautiful I am, or how nervous he was at going to a strange part of London. Literally anything. Instead he threw a tantrum. After he actually stamped his feet and shouted, "But I want to fuck you! I want to!" I told him he needed to go.

He didn't. He went and sat in front of me and muttered to himself. I was so furious I could hardly see.

We stayed at this impasse until the bus reached Waterloo Bridge, when I tapped him on the shoulder and told him he'd be stuck if he didn't get out here.

He heaved a noisy sigh and rang the bell, then got up and stood by the door glaring at me. When the door opened he said, "If only I had some self-respect," and got off.

o

He showed up wearing a fleece.

o

She planned to stay two weeks. We'd kept in touch all these years and I was so excited she was visiting me at last. But from the start her mood was very strange. She sucked her teeth about everything, but it wasn't just culture shock. It wasn't even that she was too afraid of the big bad foreign city to go anywhere on her own.

We ended up screaming at each other by the Tower of London to the point that the Scot shouted at us both, and sent us to a bench in Tenterden Square so we could resolve this like the adults we should have been.

There it all came out. On her first day, when I'd brought her back to the flat from Gatwick and left her alone to sleep off the jet lag while we were at work, she had gone to the loo, which was out of loo roll. She had never been so insulted. If we were in such financial trouble that we couldn't afford basics like toilet paper, we had no business living in one of the world's most expensive cities. She had gone out and found a store by herself and we hadn't even noticed. She was worried about me. We only had one bedroom. She was having to sleep on the sofa. Our lifestyle wasn't anything to be proud of.

I stopped her there. "I'm sorry about the toilet paper. But I will not be lectured about money by someone who declared bankruptcy age twenty-two."

o

He lived up to the academic stereotype by wearing a corduroy jacket with patches on the elbows. The drinks on Upper Street went well enough that I invited him back to mine, but once there he informed me that there were a lot of things he was going to be unable to do, since he was recovering from a recent pregnancy scare.

With one of his students, naturally.

o

He was standing next to me in the kitchen of the party. Without looking away from his friends, he leaned over to me and said out of the side of his mouth, "I would."

I looked at him. He still didn't look at me.

"Nah, you're all right."

o

She didn't manage any of the accounts I worked on, so although we'd made plenty of light-hearted chit-chat in passing, and spent more than one night at the same work drinks, I had never hung out with her by myself. So the day she asked me if I had any plans that evening, and if not, whether I wanted to grab a drink with her, I was pleased to be making a new friend.

We went to a wine bar in Seven Dials, where to my surprise she put her card behind the bar and ordered two glasses of champagne. "Now," she said. "My husband is out of town, and I am bored. So tonight, we're going to get you a man."

I was not a little insulted, but she would not let it drop. We argued until she said, "If you don't, I'll go to HR tomorrow and tell them you were racist to me."

I was blindsided. I had no idea what to do. And while I was stunned into silence, she took that as an opportunity to begin pointing out men. After a moment,

I said I had seen a good-looking one outside and went to collect myself.

I should have just grabbed my coat and left then, of course. But I'd never had anyone threaten my career for fun before.

When I went back inside, my colleague was leaning over to the two men at the next table. As soon as I was close, she said, "Here's who I'm talking about," and the three of them laid into me.

I am single, she and these complete strangers informed me, because of my hair, my face, my weight, my clothes, my shoes, and other things I have since forgotten. They really did insult me from my head down to my toes. And I was so angry I said nothing at all.

But then she began talking more closely to one of the men, and the other turned to me. He knew all about commitment, he said, because he was in a long-term relationship that had begun on a beach in Tenerife six weeks before. And as he expounded on all the things he could tell were wrong with me, I remembered my colleague had left her card behind the bar.

I signalled the waitress. "We'd like another bottle of champagne," I said. She smiled and brought it over.

I drank the entire bottle by myself while this stranger explained the secret to happiness. I let him talk at me about how wonderful his woman was and everything I needed to do to be half as good as her. When the bottle was done, I thanked him for the advice. Then I found my colleague, thanked her for the lovely evening, and left.

I showed up at the office the next day with enough cash to cover the entire bill. But she has yet to speak to me again.

o

After the Grand National finished, a celebrating redhead bumped into me. When he apologised, I laughed and said to think nothing of it. He asked if I wanted the carnation he was holding.

"Yes," I said, so he handed it over. I stuck it behind my ear and asked the obvious question.

"I just won," he said, "but my girlfriend there doesn't like carnations."

o

His desk was near mine for a long time. I knew he liked me because in the pub he had a tendency to slosh his drink over my breasts, but he never once made a pass. This was unusual because women of my nationality are his type. He spent months dating another American colleague, in secrecy, until the day they were caught snogging in the lift.

But they broke up, and I would bump into him out and about with other Americans, flirting like crazy with every other American, but never once a sniff at me.

A while after he left for a new job, he showed up at the local with his new one. When the brick shithouse cornered her, I seized my chance.

"Look, I'm not making a move. But the whole time I've known you I've watched you crack on to every other American within five miles of here except me. Why not?"

He choked on his drink hard enough that I had to slap him on the back. Once he recovered, he shook his head and said, "I thought you were Canadian."

o

His phone rang. We looked at it, then he quickly scooped it up and got out of bed.

The name that had flashed up was Munter.

o

After the tantrum-throwing redhead exited the night bus, I texted the friend from work who'd brought me to the party to apologise and tell her everything.

I didn't find out the rest for a few months.

She'd thought it was hilarious and passed her phone

27

around so everyone could read my texts and have a good laugh.

Then the redhead had showed back up. He was greeted with some surprise, because after all had he not snuck out with me? Well yes, he'd said, but he couldn't go through with it. Halfway there I had made some really outré demands that put him off his stride.

But the capper was what he said to her as she was going home. "You should take me with you," he'd said. "I'm better than a virgin."

o

The chat was going all right until I asked what his hobbies were. He texted back, "Honestly? Catfishing on Grindr."

o

I'd arranged to meet some friends at a pub in Greenwich, and got there first. It was crowded like all river pubs, so when I saw a free spot I asked the people at the table if I could sit there for a bit.

They recoiled. Then one of them said, "Do you have friends coming? It's just we don't want to be saddled with a weirdo."

o

We were fooling around and he complimented my breasts. I thanked him.

But then he said, "They are so good I think I am going to name them."

"Please don't."

He started laughing and said, "I'll call this one Hepzibah, and that one, hmm. Percival."

o

We had not yet uncoupled when he said, "I think you're great, but I should warn you. I'm not the type who commits."

o

We'd met at a party and become lively Facebook friends. When it turned out we were going to the same protest march, we decided to march together.

Afterwards we ended up on one of the beer boats in the Thames. I was surprised he'd suggested it but it was a lovely summer's day and we'd managed to find seats, so I was happy it was turning into a date. He told me all about his second home in the south of France and the secret garden he helped with in his part of London. He invited me to both of those places. We could have picnics, he said. I said I'd be delighted.

As it started getting dark he told me about how, as a younger man, he had fallen in love with a woman who dumped him before she emigrated. He had made such a scene she told him not to contact her for five years. So he waited. He saved up his money and when the time came, he flew halfway across the world to reclaim her. Only she was married, a mother, with another one on the way. She was horrified he had come. It had broken him, he said. He would never be able to love again.

"What about me?" I said.

"What about you?" he said.

"Oh come on," I said. "This date is going pretty well, don't you think?"

I have never seen anyone's mood shift so fast. His posture went from slumped over to puffed out as he said, "What? Jesus Christ. You think this is a date? This isn't a date. You thought I fancy you? Oh my God. You thought I could fancy you?"

And as if that wasn't enough, he started to laugh.

o

We met in a coffee shop in Brockley and spent about ninety minutes together, during which she told me nine times that she wasn't an alcoholic.

o

We had a couple of dates, which were fine. She was a very politically active lesbian, working for international agencies on human rights issues, and while my queerness is very real and important, I am not that gung-ho. It meant I wondered what she saw in me. It turned out she was new in town and hoping I could integrate her into the scene. She also, in every single one of her texts, pretended to be a robot.

"Boop beep," she'd add. "Beep boop."

o

He handed me my first drink and asked when I did anal.

o

The Scot badgered me until I agreed to join him and some of his schoolfriends on a camping weekend up in the Highlands. But during the hike up to the campsite I got separated from them, and then very badly lost. By nightfall I'd figured out my phone was not with me because it was in the glove compartment of the hire car. I had to spend the night out in the open. But eventually I found civilisation again.

I had been reported missing, and flyers had been made for the local area using my Facebook photos. The

Scot had supplied my personal details. He got my age and eye colour wrong, couldn't remember the clothes I was wearing, and described my body type as "not obese".

o

I couldn't understand why the bloke on the beer boat had been so awful until the leaving do of the colleague who'd taken me to Hackney. We got rid of the brick shithouse and got so drunk together we reached the stage of brutal honesty.

I asked why she'd taken so long to tell me about the redhead. She said she was worried I'd be mad at her. I assured her I'd never. But I did wonder why she never dated.

She burst into tears. "I can't. I could never fancy anyone with the bad taste to fancy me."

o

We'd spent a nice night together and were texting on and off in the days that followed. I was out in Elephant the following weekend when I noticed a missed call from him. I made my excuses to my friends and stepped outside.

He said, "Oh God, thanks for the call. It's been bothering me. I've got to tell you, I think you're great, but it's important you know I could never have any real feelings for you."

I sighed and said, "Okay?"

"So we can still be friends?" he said.

I breathed in and out again through my nose. "Sure."

He sighed with relief. Through the phone I could feel him smiling that this difficult thing had gone the way he'd wanted it to. "That's great! So what did you think of last week's *Doctor Who*?"

o

The bus was stuck in traffic, which gave us a good long view of an older couple snogging away at the stop. It is not a sight you often see, and I could feel the mood around me lighten as we all watched. The traffic moved, the bus pulled up, the woman got on and the man stood by waving.

But then the woman turned her attention to replacing her card in her bag. As soon as she looked away from him, the man flicked her the V-sign with both hands.

I wasn't the only person who lurched back in their seat.

o

He begged me to break his dry spell, and I thought, 'Oh, all right.'

We met up in an old-school boozer near his flat in Leytonstone, and he was so nervous I thought we might as well not linger. As we were walking back to his, I

33

asked him to pay me a compliment.

"No," he said. "I am terrible at it."

This was not what I wanted to hear, but you're supposed to give people a chance. "Try."

"I don't know what to say."

"You like me because I am..."

He spluttered and flailed until he said, "I like you because you're spirited."

"Like a horse."

"No! That's not what I mean. I mean, you're forceful."

"Like a rapist horse."

o

The Scot took me to a barbecue in Stoke Newington so I could meet his London friends. They weren't welcoming. Everyone kept refreshing each other's drinks but not mine. The Scot was outside somewhere, or something, when the mothers I'd been trying to chat to made a collective excuse. I found myself alone in the sitting room.

I took a few deep breaths, then got up and went outside. A few of the gang were cheering on the lads who'd found a rugby ball and were threatening the flowerbeds.

"So how long have you lived in London?" one of them said to me.

I brightened. "About fifteen years."

"Do you go home much?"

"I am home."

He snorted.

I looked at him closely and said, "Well I feel like I belong, anyway."

"You'll never sound like it, love," he said, and turned away.

o

She made a passing reference to children, which startled me, since her dating profile hadn't said anything about kids and mums usually mention them up front.

It transpired that she had three, all teenagers, all still in education, all still at home. And all three had partners. And the way her house was laid out the bedrooms were sort of like a fan, with hers in the middle, so every night she went to sleep to the sounds of her kids shagging away.

"That must make dating tough," I said.

"Oh no, they're fine with it," she said. Her phone dinged. She looked at it and laughed. "The middle one has just said I should come home. The dog misses me."

"Hmm," I said.

"Well they're still hoping I'll get back together with their dad," she said. "Although that's not going to happen. It took me a long time to accept my sexuality

35

but here I am." And she smiled.

"That must have been a big adjustment."

"Oh well, I haven't made a fuss about it. Although if they haven't figured out I'm dating women by now..."

o

His first message was, "So are you kicking ass and taking names, or kicking names and taking ass?"

o

We met at the Victoria & Albert Museum on a warm day, so I suggested going out into the courtyard. He followed as I went over to the drinks cart and picked out a lemonade.

As I paid for it, I noticed he was not in the queue. "What are you getting?" I asked.

"Oh, I'm not thirsty," he said.

o

I went to Mayfair to catch up with a friend I hadn't seen in a while. After a few drinks she asked how it was going with the Scot. I said we seemed all right, sort of, but we had probably almost definitely moved in together too soon.

She agreed but told me to be grateful I didn't have her problem.

The week before at work drinks she had spent the night flirting with the bloke who sits next to her. At closing time, they decided why not. They staggered over the road to a famously expensive hotel and he put his credit card down. They went upstairs and were getting down to it when the bloke suddenly froze. She acted out for me how he smacked his forehead and said, "I forgot to phone my wife."

Once I'd stopped laughing, I asked, "Did you know he was married?"

"No ring, and he'd never mentioned it."

"Christ."

"So it's very awkward in the office right now."

o

We agreed: the problem was the six words. Never say six words to someone.

I forgot to phone my wife

You should go back to him

I'll shove it up your shitter

I wanted you to be comfortable

My ex has a hostile uterus

For starters, it has excellent CCTV

You just have lumpy breasts, love

Oh, I hadn't thought of that

It looks like you're judging me

You could always move in here

So we can still be friends

I'm sorry about the toilet paper

But all my stuff is there

Would I have something to read

People don't normally act like this

I like you because you're spirited

If only I had some self-respect

Have you tried toning it down

Blimey, that must hurt like buggery

I bet she thought so too

Oh dear, is that your accent

You're better at this than me

I'm not the type who commits

I told you not to play

Well that was your own look-out

o

He showed up wearing a T-shirt that said SATURDAY NIGHT BEAVER.

o

We were in bed and things were not going well. I tried some stuff, but nothing was helping. After a bit we both gave up. To break the hideous silence, I said, "What's the problem?"

He shouted, "There's no problem. I just don't fancy you."

o

I had been trying to arrange drinks with the former colleague for a while, and texted suggesting a cup of coffee that weekend. She replied that she was too busy that weekend, since she had an appointment to revolutionise her hair.

o

The interviewer had his dog in with him, and he kept getting up to let it in or out. Eventually the dog stayed gone and he actually focused on my portfolio, but his tone remained condescending and I could not work out why. But you're supposed to give people a chance.

He asked about salary expectations, and I said lightly it was a bit early in the process for that.

He frowned and said that in that case he had better tell me about the company. He went on for a while about their ethos, and the creative culture which was the cause of their success. This included – and this was very important – the fact they all had the same sense of humour, an ironic and cutting one. In fact, that was their USP, this ironic sense of humour which all the employees shared.

I grinned. "Well, that might be a problem for me, since as an American I have no sense of irony."

His face fell. "Oh, I hadn't thought of that."

o

He had a tattoo of a woman's name on his arm. I didn't think much of asking whose it was.

He grimaced. "My former stepdaughter."

o

The Scot insisted I join him at a flat-warming in Wood Green with his same group of friends. The mood was strained. There was no music and everyone was sitting around looking at their knees. But you're supposed to give people a chance, so I tried hard to be engaging. After two tinnies I went to the loo and just stood there for a while, leaning against the wall.

Back in the room the mood had improved. I helped myself to another cider and realised that people were actually chatting to me.

When we were in the taxi the Scot asked if I'd noticed how everyone was nicer when I came back.

"I guess," I said.

He looked very pleased with himself. "While you were gone, I told everyone not to be the way they were to you. I said you were different. Not like other Americans."

o

I went to visit the friend with the teenage son. While she was making more tea, there was a mortified silence in the sitting room.

"Thanks for not saying anything to Mum."

"Thanks for never texting me ever again."

We nodded to ourselves.

"Things going well?"

"Yeah. I'm really happy."

"Mm. I could tell."

o

He insisted I walk him to his train. Once in Euston station he tried to convince me to buy a ticket.

I said, "You live hours outside of London."

"45 minutes direct."

"I have work in the morning."

"Trains run in the morning too."

"Tickets cost like a million pounds."

And he said, "It's not like I'm paying for it."

o

I walked into the meeting room and said, "Hello, so nice to meet you."

The interviewer said, "Oh no. Oh dear, is that your accent?"

o

He went up to Scotland for a stag weekend. Before he left he promised to call first thing Sunday morning. I pointed out he would never be in a state to. He got cross. "Woman, if I say I will do something, I will do it." I thought this was hilarious, which didn't help. It meant he phoned more on the Saturday but I didn't pick up. I was busy watching foreign films he scoffed at and romantic comedies he said were stupid.

Surprise, surprise, I had no missed calls when I woke up on the Sunday. I went about my morning – lazy coffee, Pilates class – and by the time I got home I had a single text.

"I can't believe I forgot to call the love of my life because I was passed out in a strip club."

o

I was having some pain wearing my contact lenses so made an appointment. It turned out that I had developed some infection on the underside of my eyelids.

The optometrist stepped back and looked at me. "Blimey, that must hurt like buggery."

o

A few of the women from work and I went for a prosecco. When I left the bar in Goodge Street it wasn't late but busy out. As I turned for the station a man passing spat across my path.

I didn't break stride as I said, "Oh, that's nice."

He roared, "You fucking whore. The fuck you think you are, talking to me. Do that again. I'll shove it up your shitter."

o

The power went out in the pub in Bermondsey and almost immediately staff came around with tealights. One of them said to us, "Ooh, it's romantic," as she left some on our table. "It is romantic," he said to me. "It's the perfect setting for me to tell you all about my true love."

It was a real person. She lived in Barcelona and had for over a decade. She was married to someone else and currently pregnant with her husband's child, but he was really excited about being involved in the baby's life. He could never have had a child with her himself, he said, because the sex he'd had with her was the worst of his life.

I ate another chip. "I bet she thought so too."

O

He insisted on a lunch date, and you're supposed to give people a chance. On the day itself I'd had the morning from hell so showed up in a dreadful mood. I apologised repeatedly, but he said it was no problem and then set about cheering me up, which he actually did. When the bill came, he refused to let me see it. He said it was the least he could do. As he paid, I tried to remember the last time a bloke had picked up the cheque. When I couldn't, I asked if he wanted my number.

He said no. I winced, but figured this was on me.

The next time I went into the dating app there was

a new message from him. He said he didn't know why he'd refused my number, but he had an idea of how I could make things up to him. He gave me his address, down to the flat number and the entry code for the building, and told me to present myself there at noon the following day so for lunch he could eat me.

o

One of my film friends suggested a movie-themed speed dating night. I balked, because the previous time I'd done speed dating nine men had commented on my accent before the tenth said something unrepeatably racist. But her marriage had blown up and I wanted to be supportive.

It was a wash. Hardly any men showed up and the ones who did were unusually crass, because they thought we women didn't have much choice. But the worst was while we were all mingling around awkwardly chatting, when one of them gave me a flyer for the movie-themed pub quiz he ran.

I looked at the picture. "I love Louise Brooks."

He was shocked (shocked!) that I knew who Louise Brooks was. He was not impressed or intrigued. He was angry that I understood his clever reference. My friend tried to stop me, but I discussed Louise Brooks' movies in the order of how much I like them as he got more annoyed. Once I exhausted my knowledge I added, "But she's no Clara Bow."

"Who?"

o

His first message was, "Do you like whales? Fancy a humpback at mine?"

o

One of his profile photos showed him laughing in front of a painting of Sylvester Stallone. This seemed like a good opener, so I messaged how much I like the *Rocky* films. He immediately asked which one was my favourite. You're supposed to give people a chance, so I said *Creed*.

His reply was swift. Even over text I could feel his contempt. He said its whole concept was misguided, because Apollo Creed would never have cheated on his wife. I said, "Be that as it may, it's a good premise. The film is worth it."

He called me an ignorant bitch and blocked me.

o

He told a detailed anecdote about going to Florida to

47

meet some people he knew through a message board. While he was there his friends made sure he did all the American things, like fire a gun and eat at a breastaurant. That was the only time he'd ever left the UK, but he couldn't wait to go back.

"Are you well-travelled?" he asked me.

"Not really," I said. I then listed the different countries I have lived in and every place I have visited.

When I was done, he said, "You really should travel. It broadens the mind."

o

When I refused to give him my number, he called me a cunt.

o

I went for a picnic in Regent's Park with the film friend I most admired. We analysed the latest releases until I said I needed to tell him about the epiphany I'd had the dozenth time watching *Spectre*.

Bond films are not action movies. They are romantic fantasias for men. Think about it, I said. In a world where men outsource their responsibilities, here is a man who does stuff himself. No matter where James Bond is, he knows exactly what to do.

He can speak any language, drive a speedboat, rescue somebody, fight anyone with any weapon. And he is such an immortal fuck that women don't mind that they're seen as disposable and interchangeable. He's worth it. But despite his casual attitude to sex and the ease with which he gets it, copious amounts of sex with randoms isn't what Bond really wants. All he wants is love. In every single movie, Bond acts out of love. It's not about 'Queen and Country,' not really. Look at him and Moneypenny. This is the greatest achievement of the Daniel Craig Bonds, how he's a big softie really. Everything he does is for Vesper, Camille and Fields, Séverine and M, or – most recently – Madeleine. And even though Bond is desperate to find someone who will love him back, he never, ever lies. He tells the truth about who he is and what he does. That combination of confidence, self-awareness and responsibility – which is what people mean when they say 'be a man' – is so rare, it's unbelievably hot. This is why women love Bond movies too. Best of all: Bond is not a superhero! He is just a regular hero! He's an ordinary extraordinary man, no powers, no CGI, which makes it even hotter!

Then I paused for breath and asked this man I admired what he thought. He rubbed his throat and said, "Honestly? I hate you."

The smile slid from my face as he continued, "You're better at this than me. It's not right."

o

He came home and showed me the keys for the flat he'd purchased in Glasgow. He'd had it with London; he was moving back permanently. He'd cancelled the tenancy on the flat we were sitting in and arranged to work remotely at his job.

And he had done all of these things without telling me.

I hit the roof, and he said, "Well it's not like you have a real career. Why won't you come with me?"

o

I was crashing in a friend's spare room and feeling very much in crisis. Then I discovered a lump in the breast tissue in my armpit. After many tears, and learning how long it would take to get an NHS referral, I remembered I had private health insurance through work.

A few days later I went by myself to a private hospital, where I had to take my shirt and bra off in a room full of men to have the ultrasound.

After a little while, the technician laughed. "There's

nothing for you to worry about," he said. "You just have lumpy breasts, love."

o

I asked if he'd seen any good movies lately.

He smiled unpleasantly before saying, "*Human Centipede Three.*"

o

He gave me a goodbye kiss in the middle of King's Cross so he could rub his erection against my leg.

It took me a fortnight to realise I should have said, "Aw, three quarters."

o

I met up with the friend who'd had the bad night in the hotel. I told her I was feeling quite low. I knew for sure being single again was the right decision but nothing good was happening. Nobody I met was being cool. I didn't want much, I said, but even my low expectations were too high. These days no one wants a proper relationship. I've tried so hard to give people a chance, to pretend they're engaging in good faith, and where has it gotten me. On first dates they do this. In first messages. No one asks themselves what they've got to offer. All they think about is what they want. And because they're so selfish, they think they can say or do any nasty shit they want. Like I'm a free therapist, or a mechanic repairing old bangers for fun. Just the idea I might want something is too much. When I ask for anything, they lose their minds. What happened to everybody? When did relationships, even ones that only last one night, stop being human? When did the only choice become sidekick or superhero? No one wants an equal relationship except for people already with someone. If only they grasped the irony of that. And let's not even get into splitting the cheque. Although we have to, because when these dates don't immediately get exactly what they want, they get mean. And everyone feels entitled to a hell of a lot. I stopped asking people out because they thought a woman asking meant a sure thing, that just by showing up they were guaranteed a blowjob at least, because I wouldn't have asked to meet them if I wasn't automatically up for it. So they think they don't even need to be polite, much less good in bed. Why is it such a bad time for human relationships? All that I wanted since becoming single again was to have a fun time sleeping around, and that was impossible. And the worst part was, despite all these failures and disappointments, I didn't think I was the problem.

My friend put her hand on my arm. "Well, aren't you?"

I looked at her. "Excuse me?"

She took her hand away. "I mean, you're a little much. Have you tried toning it down? Men will treat you better if they think you're dumber than them."

I couldn't believe what I was hearing. "And what, exactly, am I supposed to tone down?"

o

When I said I was divorced, he perked up and said he was too, and didn't I hate weddings now. I asked what he meant.

He said, "Isn't it awful? Don't you hate watching them say those vows and spend all that money when you know love is a lie?"

o

It was late and I had my earbuds in at the bus stop. A man came up, made eye contact and asked what I was listening to. He seemed open and friendly, so I pulled out an earbud and offered it to him. He made small talk and I told him all about why TV on the Radio are my favourite band.

My bus came and he followed me on it, flirting like

crazy. This was fine. I put my phone away and asked his name. As we introduced ourselves, we shook hands, which was when I clocked his wedding ring.

He got off at my stop and kissed me. 'What the hell,' I thought, and let him snog my face off at the well-lit bus stop on the main road.

Eventually he pulled back and said, "How about it?"

"Excuse me?"

He waved vaguely around and said, "You know. How about it?"

I stared at him. I asked if he was actually asking me to have sex with him at a well-lit bus stop on a main road. He shrugged. I told him to fuck off. He indicated the bushes with his thumb. I told him, this time with feeling, to fuck off. He asked if he could come back to mine.

I thought fast. "Okay. You wanna come back to mine? Tell me my name."

He straightened up and said, "Tell me mine."

"Your name's Steve, Steve," I said. "You told me on the bus, right before I told you mine. Come on. What is it?"

He hemmed and hawed and said, "Imogen?"

I stepped back, pointed with my whole arm, and said, "Go home to your wife!"

o

"Are you a dog or a cat person?" he asked. Without waiting for my answer, he added, "I don't like dogs myself. There was an incident when I was a kid."

"Oh yeah?"

"Yeah. My mother took me to visit some of her friends. They had a big dog, and it knocked me over. Ever since then I don't like dogs."

"That must have been upsetting. Were you badly bitten?"

"Oh no, it just knocked me over. I don't remember it, but my mother does. She doesn't like dogs anymore either."

o

I thought the date on Brick Lane was going well until he said, "Let's play who had the worst breakup."

"Absolutely not."

"Oh, come on," he said. "I bet I'll win."

"Do not do this."

"Come on, let's play. My ex got pregnant by somebody else."

I crossed my arms and said, "You wanna play? All right. We'll play." And I told him exactly why I left my husband. I made sure to dwell on the hospital part. His mouth dropped open.

When I was done, he wouldn't look at me. Eventually I said, "I told you not to play."

And all he had to say for himself was, "She had an abortion in the end."

o

She said we couldn't go back to hers because she was still living with her wife. And their toddler.

o

I met a friend I'd hadn't seen in years and his new wife for dinner. It turned out she was pregnant so they weren't drinking, but didn't mind at all if I did. I said in that case I was still ordering a bottle of wine. I asked about the baby and the new house they were renovating, but they didn't want to bore me with their dull married problems. They wanted to hear all about my exciting single life.

I'd thought I was there for dinner, instead of to be the show. But I told them about the gruesome breakup with the Scot and how dating since then was a massive letdown. I was really starting to think I'd never be anyone's precious cargo. Then I touched on my lack of success with the job hunt, but at least my new flat wasn't too grotty. Then things dragged a bit until I asked how they'd met.

They perked up and went into detail about how sad and depressing their lives had been when they were single, and how wonderful their courtship had been. Then they pulled up the wedding videos on their phones, and I kept quietly drinking. After the topic was exhausted, the wife asked what I would be doing for Christmas. I said I had no idea.

She actually put her hand to her chest. "You are so brave," she said. "I don't know how you do it. It is my worst nightmare, being alone, like you are, and having to work, like you do, and not even having anyone to take care of you –"

Her husband interrupted. "I'll always take care of you, baby."

They started snogging right there, in the middle of the restaurant.

I looked at my glass and finished the bottle.

o

It was very late in Canary Wharf and I was buying a round of vodka crème de menthes for some reason. They were so expensive that as I typed in my PIN I said to myself, "It's a good thing I'm drunk or I'd be upset about this."

As I handed round the drinks the others looked to the brick shithouse, who asked me what the work fancy was like in bed.

It stung to learn my crush was not as secret as I'd

thought. It stung worse to admit, even to myself, that he was sleeping with the Romanian girl in marketing, but I'd figured that out on my own. So I could only tell the truth.

"I've never slept with him."

They were electrified. "He's gay?"

And as they voiced their shock that we had a gay colleague in our midst, I said, "Wait a second. Is he gay because I haven't slept with him, or is he gay because he hasn't slept with me?"

o

A disturbing selfie of her appeared in my feed. I didn't know what to make of it but as we hadn't spoken for a while, not since she'd revolutionised her hair, I thought it best not to do anything.

A little later someone from her new job got in touch. The disturbing selfie was her suicide note. She'd swallowed some pills and posted it. When she didn't show up for work for a few days, they'd gone round and found her.

Her phone was still in her hand.

o

I met the friend who didn't like me in a skirt at the cinema. He'd bought only his ticket, and since it was a crowded showing nothing could be done to enable us to sit together. This was annoying but I was just happy to see him. We agreed to meet afterwards in the usual pub.

The movie was good and I enjoyed it. But when I got to the pub I couldn't find him, so I called.

"Why are you bothering me?" he said. "The movie was garbage so I cycled home. I've been here an hour."

o

I was looking forward to meeting him until he messaged, "I just gotta check one thing. Are you gonna steal my sperm?"

"What?"

"You're a woman of a certain age and we all know what that means. You're not gonna, are you?"

I looked at my phone for a while before messaging back, "Not yours."

o

The work fancy asked me to schmooze a new client with him at a mixer on the King's Road. It turned out the evening was aimed at Americans new to London. One of them bought me a beer, and as I accepted it the work fancy winked and ditched me.

I gritted my teeth and asked the one who'd bought

my drink where he had, in the American sense, gone to college.

He'd gone to Texas, he said. Best college in the world. He'd loved it there and had had a great time. Everything about it was great. He was a longhorn through and through. In fact, he was such a longhorn that for years his party trick was taking a wire hanger and shaping it into the longhorn logo. In fact, when a party was really a rager, he would heat up the longhorn-shaped wire hanger on the oven burners and brand people on the ass. In fact, there was one party where that was all he did, brand people on the ass. Best party of his life.

o

For a second date he suggested meeting at a Michelin-starred restaurant in Kensington. I was a bit surprised by the choice but didn't mind seeing him again.

As the night wore on I was disappointed by my surprise. The glam location convenient for the tube back to his was supposed to guarantee him sex. And once it became clear his moves weren't working, he spent the rest of the meal being rotten to me.

We split the cheque, so the unpleasantness at the end was limited to him kissing me outside the station, then stepping back and saying, "Wow, that was awful. You're really bad at this."

I replied, "Likewise."

o

I was on the bus when a very odd pair sat down in front of me. As I eavesdropped it became clear she was some kind of social worker escorting him to an appointment. She worked hard to make polite conversation, but it was painful. He could not remember the ages of his children, and when she asked about his hobbies, he shrugged and said, "Drinking, pet."

But then she asked about his flat, and suddenly he wouldn't shut up. He lived in the worst bedsit in the whole city, full of black mould and damp. The toilet leaked, the heating was broken, it was incredibly expensive, and it was haunted. There were ghosts hanging over his bed in the night who made it impossible for him to sleep. He was thinking of getting one of the local witch doctors around.

The social worker asked, "If it's that bad, why don't you find somewhere else?"

He shrugged again. "I would," he said, "but all my stuff is there."

o

I found out the Scot was back together with the woman he moved to London for when he posted a baby picture of her on his Instagram.

o

How long does it take to get a refrigerator delivered?

o

We'd chatted well enough in the dating app that I'd decided to break my only rule and give him my number without meeting him first. There was lots of texting and even some long phone calls, so I'd thought it would be fine to spend our first date on a dirty weekend at his.

However. While we had talked quite a bit about BDSM it had not gotten clear in my head that, for him, this was the only thing. He flatly refused to do what he called 'vanilla stuff' and I just as flatly refused to allow him to tie me to his bedposts and fuck me up the arse. But he lived ages from the night tube and didn't offer to call me a minicab, so I decided to trust that his preoccupation with consent meant that I was safe.

I was, physically. He ordered us a takeaway, food

he insisted I had to try although I'd said I didn't like it. Then we watched a movie, one he said I needed to see to be a true connoisseur, especially since none of my own suggestions were any good. I kept my temper along with one eye on the time and slept on the sofa.

The next morning, I convinced him to make me a second cup of coffee. Once he did, he went over to a wall of storage shelving and took down a nondescript plastic box. He put it on the table, pulled off the lid, and I coughed. He smirked as he dug through a startling array of vibrators and dildos, female condoms, butt plugs of increasingly alarming sizes, and several different kinds of handcuffs, because there was something he needed me to see.

Though I insisted I was fine, he pulled out a set of hand shackles on a ten-foot chain and a gas mask. With quite the glint in his eye he told me about a woman of his acquaintance whose kink was sensory deprivation. What he would do was strip her naked, put the gas mask on her, have her stand in the middle of his sitting room and shackle her hands overhead, with the chain over his ceiling beam.

I was suddenly very aware his flat had ceiling beams.

He demonstrated the position as he explained that he would leave her there for a few hours, as he ran errands or just had a few pints down the pub, while she waited in hot naked sensory deprivation for him to come back and fuck her senseless where she stood.

He looked at me in a way which made the question obvious but asked it anyway.

I looked at the gas mask.

I looked at the ceiling beam.

I looked at the shackles.

I had some more of my coffee.

I looked at him.

I said, "Would I have something to read?"

o

I hadn't seen the work fancy for a while when he materialised next to my desk because he needed me, urgently. I followed him into an empty meeting room wondering if my chance had come around at last. As he closed the door he began chuckling and said, "While it was happening, I kept thinking, 'I know who's gonna want to hear about this!'"

The fancy had, to put it delicately, injured his lower portions. He had been off sick with said injuries for the last couple of days, but refused to seek medical attention until the Romanian girl from marketing threatened to move out. So he had taken himself off to the minor injuries unit, where after a punishing wait he was summoned by a nurse.

As I digested the news that they were living together now, he acted out for me the thorough inspection he had undergone at this nurse's cold hands. Then he explained how he was lying on his stomach when the nurse snapped on a pair of gloves and said, "I require access to your rectum."

And as he gleefully described to me how he'd shed a single hot tear, I said to myself, "Never say six words to someone. Once you do, it's all over."

o

I met someone I liked and was happy with. We were at it and it was good. I was enjoying myself so I laughed.

He stopped, put his hand over my mouth, looked me in the eyes and said, "You ruin it when you talk."

o   o   o